Vain Dorothy-Jane

written by
Julie Fulton

illustrated by
Jona Jung

Miss Dorothy-Jane was ever so vain.

She stared in her mirror for hours.

Was her hair brushed just right? Was her jumper too tight?

Would her hat look much better with flowers?

When she went into town she would **strut** up and down,
thinking people would see her and smile.
That they'd say with delight, "What a **wonderful** sight
to see somebody dress with such style."

It was sunny and so she decided to go
for a stroll to the town's brand new hall.
She could see a large crowd, people shouting out loud
at a poster nailed up on the wall.

OSSIP'
QUARE.

It said, 'Hamilton Shady will need its best lady
to curtsey and welcome the Queen.
If you think you're the best, come along with the rest
and join the parade on the green.'

A dress or a skirt? Her red blouse or a shirt?
Off she rushed to pick out a new bow.
Her pink or blue shoes? There was so much to choose,
but at last she was ready to go.

Feeling sure she would win, she jumped out of her skin
when a seagull swooped over her head.
It pooed as it passed, but she stepped aside fast
so it splattered the pavement instead.

Dressmaker

ZOO

As she walked by the zoo a sea lion named Lou
flipped his fish really **high** in the air.
"Put your parasol up," shouted Keeper McCrupp,
"or it's going to land in your **hair!**"

LOU

She straightened her hat, crept around a black cat,
stepped with care past a fresh-painted seat.
Then a sports car roared by, sending water sky high.
It came splashing down right by her feet.

ZOO

Miss Dorothy-Jane, who was ever so vain,
checked herself from her head to her toes.
"I mustn't be late or arrive in a state!"
But, on turning the corner, she froze.

In the pond, on a log, was a little black dog.
It was trembling and shaking with fear.
It fell in with a yelp so she shouted out, "Help!"
But none of the people could hear.

"Oh my goodness," she cried, as she watched from the side,
"there really is no time to lose.
The dog's starting to sink." Without stopping to think,
Miss Dorothy kicked off her shoes.

HOW TO SWIM like a frog

"The poor dog will drown!" she cried out with a frown
and forgot the **parade** on the green.
She **dived** in, pulled it out, and then started to **shout**,
"I don't think I will ever get clean!"

She sat down in tears, but soon heard lots of cheers.
"We choose you to welcome the Queen.
You've got weeds on your toes, mud and slime on your nose,
but you're the best person we've ever seen!"

Miss Dorothy-Jane was no longer so vain.
She made lots of new friends in the town.
They all shouted "Hooray!" when she gave the bouquet
and the Queen smiled from under her crown.

The End

Vain Dorothy Jane

An original concept by Julie Fulton

© Julie Fulton

Written by Julie Fulton

Illustrated by Jona Jung

Published by MAVERICK ARTS PUBLISHING LTD

Studio 3A, City Business Centre, 6 Brighton Road,

Horsham, West Sussex, RH13 5BB

+44 (0)1403 256941

© Maverick Arts Publishing Limited

Published March 2016

*A CIP catalogue record for this book is available
at the British Library.*

ISBN 978-1-84886-198-5

Maverick
arts publishing
www.maverickbooks.co.uk